TILLY'S *Animal* ADVENTURE

WRITTEN & ILLUSTRATED BY

Stephenie Poeschel

IN A TOWN IN WISCONSIN,

WITH ENDLESS BLUE SKIES,

LIVED A LITTLE GIRL NAMED TILLY,

SO SWEET AND SO WISE.

TILLY LOVED HER DOG,

SHE THOUGHT GUS WAS SO GRAND,

BUT SHE ALSO KNEW THAT OTHERS,

COULD BE FOUND ACROSS THE LAND.

WITH A HEART FULL OF WONDER,

SHE SET OUT ONE SUNNY DAY,

TO EXPLORE THE WHOLE WORLD

IN HER OWN SPECIAL WAY.

IN HER GREEN HELICOPTER,

SHE PREPARED HERSELF TO FLY,

IN SEARCH OF THE BEST ANIMAL,

IN LAND AND SEA AND SKY.

HER FIRST STOP WAS IN BELGIUM
WHERE SHE SAW A SIGHT SO RARE,
CLIMBING HIGH UPON A MOUNTAIN
WAS A BROWN GRIZZLY BEAR.
HE LOOKED KIND OF SCARY,
WITH SHARP TEETH AND A SCOWL,
TILLY SCURRIED OFF
WHEN SHE HEARD HIS BIG LOUD GROWL!

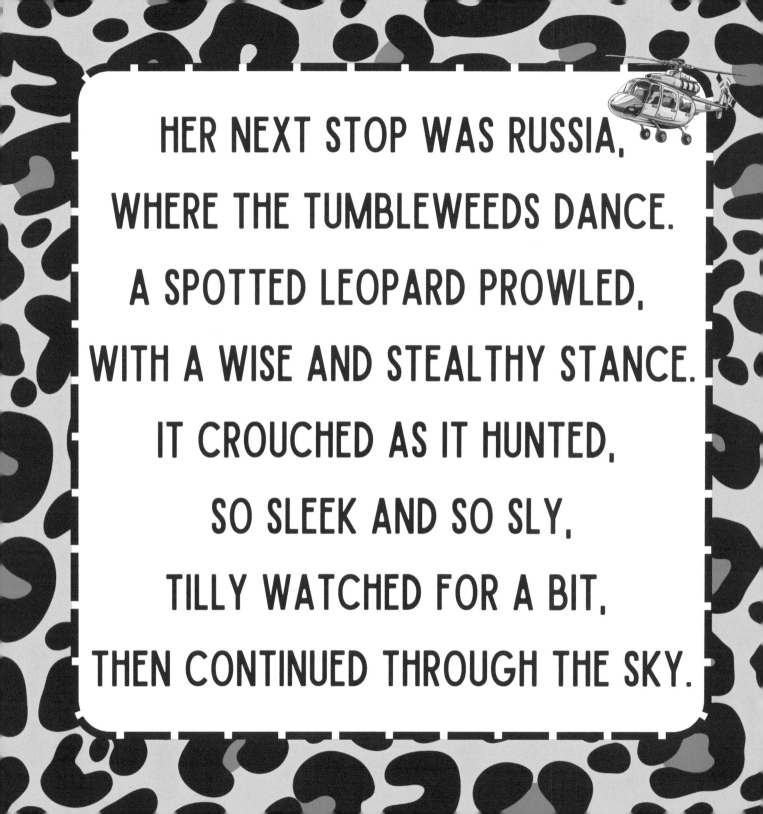

HER NEXT STOP WAS RUSSIA,
WHERE THE TUMBLEWEEDS DANCE.
A SPOTTED LEOPARD PROWLED,
WITH A WISE AND STEALTHY STANCE.
IT CROUCHED AS IT HUNTED,
SO SLEEK AND SO SLY,
TILLY WATCHED FOR A BIT,
THEN CONTINUED THROUGH THE SKY.

AS SHE NEARED INDONESIA,

SHE SAW SOMETHING SO GRAND.

A BLACK AND WHITE PANDA,

ROLLING ALL OVER THE LAND.

ALTHOUGH IT LOOKED SO SOFT,

AND LIKE IT WOULD BE FUN,

TILLY SAW ITS CLAWS

AND DECIDED SHE SHOULD RUN!

TO AUSTRALIA SHE SOARED NEXT
INTO THE SUN'S LIGHT,
WHERE A KANGAROO HOPPED,
WITH ITS JOEY TUCKED IN TIGHT.
SHE TRIED TO GET CLOSER,
BUT IT TURNED WITH A KICK,
SO TILLY GAVE UP CHASE,
AND SHE FLEW OFF VERY QUICK.

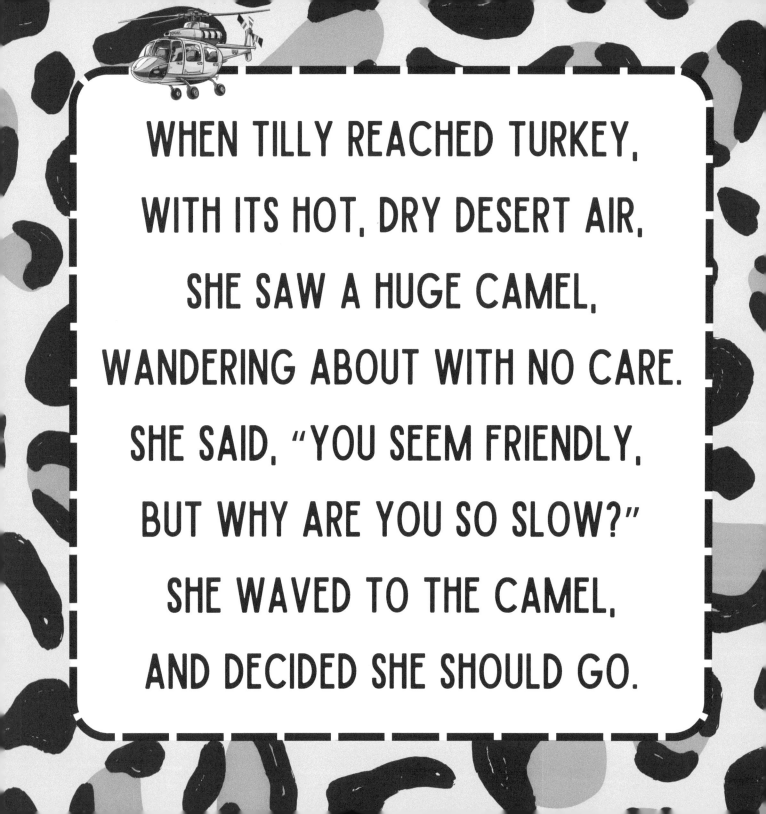

WHEN TILLY REACHED TURKEY,
WITH ITS HOT, DRY DESERT AIR,
SHE SAW A HUGE CAMEL,
WANDERING ABOUT WITH NO CARE.
SHE SAID, "YOU SEEM FRIENDLY,
BUT WHY ARE YOU SO SLOW?"
SHE WAVED TO THE CAMEL,
AND DECIDED SHE SHOULD GO.

IN AFRICA'S VAST JUNGLE,

A GIRAFFE STOOD BRAVE AND TALL,

TILLY KNEW THIS ANIMAL

WAS THE TALLEST OF THEM ALL!

SHE WATCHED HIM SAUNTER SLOWLY

AS SHE COUNTED EACH LARGE SPOT,

"YOU ARE VERY CUTE,

BUT THIS PLACE IS MUCH TOO HOT!"

SO TILLY MOVED ON,

TO A PLACE THAT WAS SO CHILLY,

AND THERE SHE SAW A PENGUIN,

WHO WADDLED AROUND SO SILLY.

SHE WANTED TO STOP AND PLAY

WITH THE YOUNG AND THE OLD,

BUT SHE SHIVERED AS SHE SAID,

"ANTARCTICA'S TOO COLD!"

TILLY FLEW NORTHWEST
TO BRAZIL'S NICE WARM WEATHER,
THERE SHE FOUND A TOUCAN,
WITH A BRIGHTLY COLORED FEATHER.

THOUGH IT HAD VIBRANT COLORS,
A TRUE SIGHT TO ADORE,
TILLY KNEW OTHER ANIMALS
THAT SHE LOVED EVEN MORE.

TILLY HAD SEARCHED THE WORLD
OVER LAND AND SHINING SEA,
DISCOVERING THE ANIMALS
THAT ROAMED SO WILD AND FREE.
FINALLY, SHE REALIZED,
WITH A SMILE AND A SIGH,
THAT SHE WAS MISSING HOME,
AND NOW SHE KNEW JUST WHY.

WITH A HEART FULL OF LOVE,

SHE KNEW THAT IT WAS TRUE,

IT WOULDN'T FEEL LIKE HOME

'TIL SHE HEARD A COW GO MOO.

SHE GUIDED HER HELICOPTER

BACK TO THE USA,

BACK TO HER FARM AND FAMILY

TO FIND HER DOG AND PLAY.

SHE SAW GUS COME RUNNING,

WITH A BARK AND A WIGGLE,

AND THEY ROLLED ON THE GROUND,

WITH A HUG AND A GIGGLE.

TILLY KNEW RIGHT THEN

THE ANSWER TO HER QUEST,

THERE WERE MANY DIFFERENT ANIMALS,

BUT HERS WERE THE BEST!

Can You Help Each Animal Find Their Home?

BROWN BEAR	PENGUIN
JAGUAR	TOUCAN
KANGAROO	PANDA BEAR
COW	GIRAFFE

Did You See The Helicopters?

TILLY'S 'COPTERS ARE SCATTERED
ALL OVER THIS BOOK...
HOW MANY CAN YOU COUNT
IF YOU GO ON BACK AND LOOK?

TILLY'S *Adventure* SERIES

COMING SOON

TILLY'S TROPICAL ADVENTURE
TILLY'S CARNIVAL ADVENTURE
TILLY'S CAMPING ADVENTURE
TILLY'S FISHING ADVENTURE
TILLY'S CIRCUS ADVENTURE

AVAILABLE ON AMAZON!

Other Titles Written by Stephenie Poeschel

A BEAUTIFUL STORY OF HOPE AND LOVE FOR CHILDREN MISSING A SIBLING AT CHRISTMASTIME.

A FUN CHRISTMAS COLORING AND ACTIVITY BOOK FOR CHILDREN

PIANO STUDENT LESSON PRACTICE LOGBOOK SERIES

For Keagan, Blair, Floyd & Tilden...
May you always chase your dreams with wonder in your eyes. With all my love... Aunt Steph

If you enjoyed this book, I'd be forever grateful if you could head on over to my Amazon page and leave a positive review! Also, head on over to my website and sign up for my emails to get a notification when I release a new book! Thank you for reading!

WWW.LYLADAVISNOVELS.COM

Published by Ivory Pages Publishing.

Milton Keynes UK
Ingram Content Group UK Ltd.
UKHW052339251123
433239UK00003B/12